Murder In Hot Coffee

KT Ashely

ISBN 978-0692616451
ISBN 0692616454

Library of Congress Control Number:
2016901112

Edited by David J. Sebesta
Cover by Zach McCain

KT Ashely is the author of

The Pool,
a novella
and
Strayed and Other Stories of Life On Edge,
a collection of short stories

More from KT Ashely
www.authorktashely.com

For Miss Lynda
who by introducing me to Hot Coffee intrigued
and inspired the creation of this work.

And to Miss Gwen for her gracious sharing of
historical knowledge and reference which was
invaluable to this and future stories.

CONTENTS

MURDER IN HOT COFFEE

The caw of a crow could be heard near the street just at day break. Denia was cooking her breakfast. The daily menu routinely consisted of one egg, a slice of fried hog jowl, a kolache filled with her prize winning fig jam, and a cup of hot coffee—with *a little* homemade, vanilla tonic added for *flavor*. The smoked meat filled the house with its savory aroma as it spit and popped in the hot black iron skillet.

As the bacon continued to slowly sizzle she took the opportunity to check on her wayward cat. The woman gazed through the glass at her front door but could see nothing other than familiar obscured shapes in the night. She supposed that the crows had started early to pick her prized pecans. So she pulled back the door, creaked open the screen barrier, and stepped out onto the porch.

"Shoo! Shoo on outta here you nasty ol' things," she called out into the dark. The unseen bird went silent. She then called out "Moonshine! Moonshine! Here kitty-kitty-kitty."

Moonshine lived up to his name. When Miss Denia let him out at evening time to take care of his business, he often would not return until morning. All the neighbors knew the cat because his offspring sported some form of his white, heart-shaped patch upon his chest. This explained his habit of lying around the house all day. But when the old black tom did not answer her calls, she went back in to check on the bacon.

Once the meal had finished cooking Denia placed her prepared dish on the back porch table. Then she remembered, "Oh my coffee!" She returned to retrieve it from the stove along with a bottle of tonic from the pantry.

As she was making her way to the table she caught sight of a tall, slim, quick-moving figure out of the corner of her eye. She had not heard anyone come up from the back steps; the backyard had been quiet. In an instant the form silently appeared at her screen door beneath the shadows.

Before she could cry out a man called loudly, "Howdy-do Miss Denia. I brought your milk an' such."

Mr. Hobbes had arrived with his delivery wagon from the nearby mercantile to drop off the stores she had ordered. He made his early morning rounds every other day.

"Oh Mr. Hobbes, you just gave me a fright. You sure are early this morning. Or is it just me? I was so tired last evening that I went to bed before the chickens."

"Well ma'am, same time as always; you're second on my stop. Don't never see you up so early. Nights are getting longer ya' know."

"I suppose they are. Come on in here, Sam, and put that box on the kitchen table."

Denia took the hidden elixir from behind her back and shoved it in a covey near the door as the visitor entered. He didn't notice her stealthy way as she held the door open for him. The delivery man completed the task as he was told.

After delivering goods for Mr. Herbert's store for the past thirty years, Sam Hobbes was known as a *trusted soul*. Everything in the box was in perfect order. It contained a wedge of hoop cheese, a tin of Clabber Girl, a bottle of Bee brand vanilla extract, two shiny, new pie pans, salt, and a chunk of smoked meat. The bottle of milk was placed beside the box. He had to scoot a carving knife to the side as he slid the package over the butcher block.

"I was just gonna pour the coffee. It's steamin' hot—would you like to take a cup with you?"

"Oh, no ma'am. I don't drink the stuff. My gran'mama always said that's what made my skin so dark—my mama drank too much of it before I was born."

They laughed together and Denia placed the hot pot of coffee back on the stove. She had carried it back into the kitchen with her.

"Well, my granny told me something like that about when I was born too. She said that when my Daddy first saw me, he named me Denia because I smelled so sweet and that I was as pure white as a delicate little gardenia blossom."

Denia had told that story from time to time for many different reasons. But it was a lie. It was something made up, used this time perhaps because she felt self conscious about a hidden secret in the presence of a Negro. Her name and her own history was that of the *Saqaliba*—the Slavic slaves of the Umayyad Caliphate. The nervous tales told by the two seemed awkward but congruous. Sam Hobbes gave her a compulsory smile.

They then entered into polite conversation. Denia turned her back to him and reached for a cracker tin on a high cupboard shelf. She wore a simple cotton dress that she had made; the fabric appeared to be unseasonably thin for such a cool morning. As the woman fumbled about they discussed the humid weather and she complained that the crows were eating her pecans. She asked *how his mule Oscar was doing today* as well.

Sam continued to watch her from behind as she stretched on her toes for the container. A large bowl was nearly knocked free from its resting place. He reached out to catch it but she regained her composure and replaced the falling stoneware without his assistance.

When she turned around Sam had stepped back. The woman pulled the top from the tin exposing a thin wad of loose bills. She reached inside and gave him the money for her purchase and also the balance for the order before. Then Denia went to a corner pie safe and pulled out a small leather coin purse. He noted her slender, lily white fingers as they pulled out a shiny nickel. There was no wedding ring. It was a curiosity to him.

"This is for you, Mr. Hobbes. Maybe you can add it to your tobacco money today. And take an ol' hard pear off that tree back there for a treat for your mule."

"Why thank you ma'am. We'll sure enjoy your generosity today," the man said. And he left to continue his rounds about the small town delivering milk, dry goods and sacks of feed for the neighbor's yard fowl.

Denia could hear the crow calling as she once more retrieved the coffee pot from the stove. It irritated her—just knowing *that bird was calling his friends to come and partake in the feast*. But she sat back down to finish her breakfast while it was still hot.

She retrieved the hidden bottle and added a bit of her vanilla tonic to her cup—and then another. In all Denia had three cups of coffee although the addition of the extract infused elixir varied in strength from start to finish. Her homemade, *nervous health* concoction had been made with the mixture of a corn-based, clear liquid possibly obtained from a well known, albeit unnamed, associate of her late husband who resided further up in the county. She had been making the elixir ever since the infamous Jamaica Ginger scare in town.

The woman of not more than forty-three years in age had lost her mate to a logging accident only two years before. He was a foreman for the logging company. Unfortunately, their son was also killed working in the woods. They had no other children.

"Those dern crows. They're just gonna get all of my pecans before I can make my pies."

Denia finished her leisurely breakfast and put away the recipe notes she had been sorting through. She then marched out to check on her nut crop in the front yard. After peeking from behind the open screen door she discovered a gathering of crows pecking and poking in a circle.

"Shoo, y'all. Shoo!" she cried but the birds were not intimidated. She then pushed open the squeaky screen door and walked out unto the porch steps until they flew off.

In the new morning light she was startled to see something oddly shaped and partially covered near a patch of bear grass. It was in the corner of her front yard near the road. Investigating half way across the property she realized what the old yucca plants had been harboring. It was a body.

"Murder! Murder!" she screamed. Denia ran back into the house and tapped on the phone to call the operator.

"There's a murder in my front yard!" she told the woman. "Call the sheriff! Call him now!"

The excited woman hurried back to her breakfast sanctuary and brooded over another cup of coffee and then another. By the time the sheriff had traveled from Collins she had downed a sixth cup for the morning.

Sheriff Henry was a handsome man. He had known Denia since childhood. She had married one of his best friends; but he had never told her of his feelings for her. And the man never married despite the many opportunities given him by eligible maidens. He had moved to the larger town and concentrated on a lawman's career when Denia and her new husband traveled to Turkey as missionaries. They had been witnesses to some of the atrocities of the Armenian massacres.

"Oh Albert, look what's happened. How awful," she exclaimed.

The man took note of her sweet smelling vanilla-breath. Denia had always been just as her daddy had said—*a delicate little blossom with a sweet fragrance about her.* He also noticed the flush about her face. It was *the color of blush like that of a Confederate Rose* he thought.

The Sheriff looked the body over. He carefully lifted it up by the shoulders and the head drooped haphazardly. "Must have had his neck broke," he stated matter of factually.

One of the unfortunate soul's eyes was missing and his belly was partially disemboweled. The white on his chest was stained pink.

"Oh I know it was that white-trash Adeline Skrool that did this! I just know it was her!" Denia cried. "She musta been spying on me. She hates me. She's jealous because I've won so many ribbons for my jams at the fair. She's always makin' trouble!"

Denia Andersen was known as the *Fig Jam Queen* of Covington County. Although judging had always been by secret entry, her recipes had been a favorite for several years running. It seemed no one could make a jam, jelly or preserves better than her. Denia would even skip some years just to give another contestant a chance at winning the blue ribbon. But even that did not seem an equal opportunity to many of her competitors. Some complained that she should be beaten *fair and square.*

"Now Denia, I'm not too sure about that. Looks like old Moonshine could've been run over by a wagon or a work truck carrying some of those WPA boys over to the new road. And the crows probably did the damage to the rest of the body. Without you seeing what happened here, and if no one comes forward—that will have to be the consensus as far as I'm concerned."

"Well whoever did it you just need to round 'em up and take 'em across the river to string 'em up in Cracker's Neck!"

The distraught woman broke down sobbing loudly. The sheriff put his arms around her to offer her comfort. He could feel her hot skin upon his body and he soon surmised her intoxicated state.

"Com'on, Miss Denia. Let's get ya' back up in the house so you can lie down. I'll get a stitch of burlap and take care of ol' Moonshine. I'm afraid the only witnesses to this murder may well have been *a murder of crows.*"

Sheriff Henry saw it fitting to bury the old tomcat between two clumps of Denia's Angel's Trumpets. As he shoveled the last pile of dirt over the grave he noticed one of the big black birds perched on the town sign that read *Welcome to Hot Coffee*. It remained there and stared silently back at him until he finished his work and drove off.

The woman had fallen asleep on her fainting couch once the sheriff had placed her there. She slept peacefully until noon. He had covered her gently with her granny's afghan. All was quiet again. But the gathering of crows returned to feast on Denia's pecans as she slept.

ANGEL'S TRUMPET

When Angel's Trumpet that you see,
Jump back fast as can be.
If you touch it you will see
The Angel of Death coming for Thee.

The air had cooled in the few days since the murder of Moonshine. Denia still mourned the loss of her cat but she had no clue as to what had happened to him. It was a blur. It was as if she could not remember anything about it.

The only thing she was sure of was that the cat had gone missing. And that her neighbor Hannah told her that he had been struck by a passing truck or wagon. The neighbor also relayed the news that Sheriff Henry had buried the *poor creature* between her Angel's Trumpets on the side of the house. But she could remember none of it.

Denia thought about these things as she picked wild persimmons on the edge of her back property. The wood line thickened as it went in. Only an old Indian trail led back there. Further on was the river and a swamp once used by the Newt Knight gang to hide out from bounty hunters.

As the woman faced the forest picking fruit a man emerged. It was if he had appeared from a concealing mist, yet the day was clear and bright. Denia emptied the ripe orange bulbs from her apron into a basket on the ground.

"Halito, chim achukma?" the man greeted. His hair was a coarse black. It had two long braids in back but the front bangs were cut straight across and above his eyebrows.

"Um achukma hoke! Chishnato?" Denia replied.

"I am doing well also." The man stated.

"I'm picking some fruit to make my persimmon butter," Denia said as he neared her. "I will have some for you soon."

"It is always a pleasure to receive such a gift. But today I bring one for you."

The man reached into a leather skin satchel that was slung over his shoulder. His skin was dark *like burnt red clay* Denia thought. His features were much like Mr. Hobbes but his face more chiseled with high cheekbones.

He retrieved a small quart sized and woven cylinder basket from his bag. It was made from bear grass; inside was a burnished black jar made of clay. The top was covered with the same unwoven, green yucca leaf and sealed shut with beeswax.

"Thank you my friend," Denia said. And she gave to him a replica of the same basket covered jar that he had given her. The replacement however was empty. Its open interior smelled of a strong type of corn liquor.

"How are your dreams, Denia?" the man inquired.

"They are fitful. I make the tonic but I am afraid I have forgotten the recipe my mother taught me. I seem to be more restless than before. And I cannot remember things. My cat was killed the other day and I don't remember how. My neighbor thinks I'm drinking—but I am not. I only use this with the Angel's Trumpet leaves. I have never had this reaction."

The two talked about the concoction she

had been making since she was a child. Her mother had taught her how—she had been an Isleño healer from the south of Louisiana. Denia was very familiar with natural medicines and potions.

"That is not enough of the plant to cause these types of symptoms," the man with striking amber eyes stated. "What else is happening?"

"Well, I don't feel different—just very tired a lot. Sometimes I sleep until late and other times, like I said, I can't sleep at all. But I just can't remember things. Things get misplaced."

"Dreams, Denia. Think about your dreams," the man insisted.

"Sometimes I don't dream. Other times they are fitful and I think I see things when I wake up. Or maybe I am still asleep. I'm not sure."

The man scowled. His eyes narrowed at her. He stuck out his hands as to clasp her face but held them to the side of her temples as to feel the air from between the open space.

"I do see ghosts," she added.

"Ghosts?" the man stated more than questioned.

"Yes. Sometimes when I wake up—or I

think I'm awake; I see shadow men."

The hands of the visitor dropped casually by his side. "Nalusa Falaya," he said. "And have you heard your husband call to you in the forest?"

"I-ah, uH." Denia stuttered. She paused. "Yes."

"And you went looking for him—deep in the wood."

"Yes I did. I know he's dead…but I did," she said with head bowed.

The man looked more concerned than as to have pity upon her. A tear fell from her cheek."

"Denia. This shadow man. Sometimes you feel paralyzed when you wake up and you cannot move? And sometimes you wonder if you are awake or that you are still dreaming in the dark?"

"Yes."

"It is no dream. It is the long evil one— *Nalusa Falaya*. Or even *Impa Shilup* the soul eater. Your longing for your husband and your depression has brought ill upon you."

"But Jonathan has been dead for two years. I was very depressed months ago. But I have recovered and started my life over. I have adjusted," she refuted.

The man looked into her vibrant green eyes. He continued to think to himself for several minutes. He still stared at her even as she looked down after a moment.

"Who is this that torments you so now, Denia? Who is this *woman* I *see*?"

A cool breeze blew at the back of the woman's neck. Even in the warm sunlight she still felt cold. Denia pulled her shawl over her shoulders and wrapped her arms underneath.

"Addy Skrool."

"*Skrool?* I don't know this woman. Is she near to you?" the man asked.

"Adeline Skald. Her real name is Skald. We used to call her Skrool because she was so cruel as a child. We wouldn't play with her at school much because she was always playing tricks and hurting us as kids. She used to stomp on small forest creatures. She would bring little squirrels and such to school and then kill them in front of us. By the time we were all about twelve, she started torturing dogs and cats. She's trash!"

"Skald. Yes I know that name. They live on the northern waters—on the river near the swamp's edge. Their family has been here for a long time," the man said. "But they are not native here. They are not my people; and they are the northern whites."

Denia gave him a curious look. She did not fully understand what he was saying.

"Denia? Deeenniiaaaa!" the call came from the direction of the house.

"It's Hannah. She's looking for me. I——."

But the man interrupted, "I must go. I will see you again soon."

Denia turned to the woman's voice and cried, "I'm here! I'm coming." But as she turned back again to thank the man he had already gone into the wood. It was if he was absorbed into a fog—but it was a clear day.

Denia met her friend Hannah at the landing of her back porch. The neighbor looked impatient but happy to see her. They hugged as if they were sisters.

"I'm glad to see you up and about Denia. It's nearly noon," Hannah directed.

"I'm sorry Hannah. I got up late. But I did get some persimmons. We should have enough to make the butter."

"What is that? It looks like an Indian basket of some sort."

"Oh, it's my tonic base," Denia replied as they entered through the back screen door.

"Denia. You know I don't approve. Where'd you get that from? The Redbones or even the Skalds?" she questioned sarcastically.

"No. And the proper name is name is *Melungeon*," Denia corrected.

"Well, call them what you like but they're still nigrahs."

"Melungeons are *part* nigrah—but also Indian and white. Kinda like Creoles of color. And besides—Sam Hobbes is a nigrah."

"Yeah, but old Sam is good and trustworthy. He's not like them. Those *whatever* you said are still trash just like those carpetbaggin' Skalds—and that old Addy Skrool with her *kind*."

Denia ignored her chastising friend and put the persimmons on the heavy block table before asking, "Would you like some tea? I haven't had a chance to eat breakfast yet so if you don't mind how 'bout some coffee and pecan pie?"

Under any circumstance an opportunity to sample Miss Denia's baking was good fortune indeed. Hannah did not need to be asked twice. And she figured that it would not hurt her shapely body—the reason she knew her husband had married her, or at least he teased as such. Besides, Hannah was not a huge baker although Denia was teaching her more and more about the craft.

"Yes please, I will have the pie. And the

tea. You know I don't drink coffee."

Denia opened her cupboard and pulled out a tea tin that was next to a coffee grinder, a sack of roasted beans, and coffee cups. Above the narrow shelf were a cracker tin and a large bowl. After Denia retrieved the tea and cups she put a pan of water on the stove to boil. She also put on an already prepared pot of coffee.

"Denia," Hannah asked, "Why do you always have your coffee already soaking in your pot?"

"Oh, I guess its habit. Jonathan liked it that way. He said that when you grind the beans to let the grinds soak, that way the coffee is smoother because it doesn't have to boil as long. He says the longer it steeps in the cold water the smoother it is. I just prepare it the night before. And since he likes his coffee when he comes home from work—I make it up to steep after breakfast again. Then it's ready when he gets here."

The neighbor sat quietly. After a moment Denia realized that she had been speaking as if her husband were still alive. She said to Hannah, "Grab that pie will you, Hannah?" And she pointed to the pie safe across the kitchen. She did not want her friend to see her eyes watering. But her friend knew.

Hannah served up the pie. Denia retrieved her recipe collection and poured the hot drinks. They sat at the table in the enclosed portion of the back ell. The near view from the windows gave a pleasing vista of fruit trees and fallow garden beds. Only greens and winter squash now thrived.

"Denia, I'm so sorry about Moonshine. I know you must miss him. He was with you for so many years," the woman tried to comfort.

"Yes he was. And I miss my husband." After stating that Denia reached into a small pantry near the table and pulled out a pint sized bottle of dark liquid. It smelled of vanilla as she poured some into her coffee.

"I'm sorry. I didn't mean to upset you anymore," Hannah expressed.

"No. It's OK. I have been nervous more than usual lately."

"Does that stuff help? I mean it is moonshine isn't it?" Hannah inquired thoughtfully this time.

"Moonshine? No Hannah. This is an elixir—a nervous tonic. My mother taught me how to make it." Denia paused before continuing with her thought. Then she said softly, "She was a healer. From the southern coast of Louisiana."

"A Louisiana healer? Like voodoo?" the surprised woman chirped.

"Noooo. Not voodoo," Denia replied indignantly. "She was Isleño. Her people were originally from the Canary Islands—a part of Spain. Voodoo was derived from an African religion."

"Well, I knew everyone would come to your mother when we needed a salve or cough tonic or something—but I never realized she was a real medicine woman."

"Every culture has its own healers, Hannah. My mother's people are very old. They traveled to South America and other places exploring new lands and escaped persecution—like my father's people."

"Your father? Where were his people from?"

"Bohemia. He was a Slav. They call them the "dirty whites" because their skin was darker. A more olive tone," Denia stated.

"But neither your mother or father had dark skin. And you are pale white with green eyes—though your hair *is* black."

"Yes, well, there were pale skinned Slavs and Iberians. But they were also *Saqaliba*—slaves. In many places the northern Europeans look down on us. That is why my parents moved here from Louisiana. And they changed their last name to a more acceptable sounding one. But I always felt ashamed of who I am regardless. Our customs still survive to some extent. But my parents refused to teach me their language. Now all I know are my father's recipes for cooking, and my mother's healings. And the true meaning of my name."

"Your name? I thought your father named you after a gardenia blossom."

"No. I just tell that story to cover it up. Denia is a city in Spain. There was an uprising of slaves there in the Middle Ages. Like I said, some customs still survive."

"Like that tonic you make."

"Yes, like the tonic. It is made from the leaves of Angel's Trumpet," Denia said.

"Angel's Trumpet?" Hannah cried. "That's poison!"

"Well if you misuse it is. But it's also old medicine. It helps with consumption and nervous mind," Denia shot back.

By this time Denia had begun drinking her second cup of coffee with another dose of elixir. Hannah had known her since childhood but she was beginning to feel uneasy about her friend.

"Hannah. You only use the leaves. And not

much. The alcohol helps extract the oils from the plant. If you use too much it can cause your skin to itch like crazy, and your eyes to grow wide—and hallucinations, your heart to stop, and even death. But first you start to forget things in the smaller but more potent doses. But never use the seeds—especially from the dried pods. They can be lethal even in small amounts."

"Yeah, and I've heard of voodoo queens using stuff like that to make living dead people. They're alive but when told what to do they just obey their masters without question or emotion," the frightened neighbor replied.

"That's probably made with Devil's Breath flowers. It's similar to Angel's Trumpet but comes from South American jungles. Sometimes they use a fish poison to make such potions. But that's mainly used for nervous condition too," Denia informed.

"And that is why you use it? Because you are nervous?"

"I started using it after Jonathan was killed. You remember how upset I was. It helped me relax. I found it in my mother's old recipes."

"Well I guess I can understand that. But you seem to use it a lot. That's why your breath smells like vanilla," Hannah chastised.

Denia thought about that for a second. She then replied, "When I was a little girl my mother made it with vanilla and sugar so I would drink it when I had the cough."

"Look Denia, I know it's been hard on you losing your husband and now your cat. But I worry about you. And that trashy Addy Skrool doesn't help. Is she still coming around bothering you?"

"Sometimes I see her passing by with her husband on their horse. They come up from the back woods into town."

"Well they're just trash—marrying her first cousin. And you know they all do it," Hannah stated with disgust in her voice. "Everybody knows that even the Knight rebels wouldn't have 'em. My Daddy told me they deserted from the Union aggressors to over here during the battle of Vicksburg. They say they even dynamite fish in the river.

Those boss men had no reason to make that sorry old Silas Skald foreman when Jonathon died. He didn't deserve it. But they sure found that out when they caught him stealing—fired his sorry tail. 'Least after all that my husband finally got the position like he should have."

Hannah took a dainty sip of her tea as was

her customary mannerism. Denia turned to prepare herself another cup of the coffee concoction. After Hannah had settled her anger down a bit over the thought of Silas Skald, she realized what she had just said. The young woman noticed a tear on Denia's pale face.

"Oh—honey. I'm sorry; I didn't mean…"

"It's OK, Hannah. I know you didn't. It's just that Addy had been by the house soon after to see me and *say* how sorry she was. But she boasted that her husband was now the boss and *that she would soon have enough money to be as fine a lady as I was.*

But one thing stuck in my mind about that day she visited. She said it was a bad day alright, and that *it was too bad that no one but Silas had seen what happened. It musta been a chance accident that the chains just came loose and that the logs crushed Jonathan right in front of him.*

And then she smiled. I told her to leave and never come back around here. She was always so cruel."

Denia took a long sip of the hot coffee. Hannah noticed that she was becoming less and less wrought with emotion. This time there was no tear when she reminisced about this part of the story. It worried her friend.

"Denia. There is something else I am curious about. Why don't you wear your wedding band anymore?"

"Well," the woman started, "I can't find it. I seem to be misplacing things. And the picture of Jonathon by my bed is missing. The other day I couldn't find a carving knife to cut the bacon with. I just can't remember what I did with them."

"Jonathan got that ring for you in Turkey when y'all were on missions. How could you lose that? It was one of a kind!" Hannah said alarmed.

"I don't know. I'm just not myself lately. It's been going on for a month or so now. I think."

Hannah started to wonder if Denia was going crazy or even slowly poisoning herself with the tonic due to the loss of her husband. She seemed to be tired more often and her forgetfulness was becoming noticeable.

"Well Denia, maybe we should start on this persimmon butter," Hannah encouraged.

"OK. Let me get the recipe."

Hannah looked at Denia in a curious way. She watched as her friend mindlessly rubbed her arm; Hannah had noticed before that Denia had developed this odd tic.

"Denia. It's right here." The woman appeared less coherent. "Are you OK?"

"I'm fine. I just felt a little dizzy."

Hannah could not tell if Denia was lying or if she was truly afflicted. Her eyes seemed to be wide open but her actions it seemed were not her own. She considered if her friend was intoxicated by the plant elixir or simply the liquor it contained. Either way, Hannah was frustrated with her friend's actions.

"OK, Denia. I think I'll just go home. Why don't you let me know when you are feeling better," Hannah snapped impatiently. "I'll check on you again tomorrow morning and we'll get started early. OK?"

Denia's response was impassive. Hannah exited through the ell from the kitchen. But when she turned to say goodbye to her friend Denia only stared back at her with a simple, blank smile. Hannah wondered about the woman's actions but she inferred it more as being rude. After all, she had just wasted the later part of the morning drinking tea, eating pie, and accomplishing nothing.

Denia woke from a fitful dream. The

room was dark. She could still smell the burning bodies in the street. There had been gunshots and crying. She and Jonathon had run through the streets to escape the chaos. A door burst open and a man beckoned them into safety. And although the man's skin was a familiar brown, his long black braids with trimmed bangs across his forehead were uncharacteristic for the region.

The dream was discernible. It was more of a memory. When she and her new husband had been on missions they found themselves witnesses to a massacre of Armenians they had been ministering to. As they fled the streets from oncoming soldiers a man opened his door to shelter them. It was here that they took safe harbor for several days before they were able to leave the country.

During that time the widower became fond of the couple. He noticed that Denia had no wedding band. Jonathan explained that they had no money for one and that their love was enough to satisfy any tangible symbol of their marriage. So the old man gave them his deceased wife's ring with his blessing.

The ring was like none other. It was gold and had beautiful etchings about it. Two tiny rubies were inlaid in it about the infinity knots.

Denia knew right away that the old couple had been Christian converts; Muslims would not wear such a thing.

In her waking haze Denia saw a fleeting tall shadow. "Jonathan!" she cried into the dark. But there was no response. *Perhaps it was just the ghost of a Confederate solider or Choctaw Indian. This house is old* she thought. But the feelings she often had of being watched still unnerved her.

Denia glanced at her bedside clock. The hands read a few minutes after six. She threw on a dress made of heavier fabric than that worn of days before and covered herself in a shawl. She then went downstairs to make breakfast.

When the woman got to the kitchen she noticed the persimmons and recipe notes on the block table. An unsecured spice sachet was also lying next to the fruit. Denia could not remember what she had done after Hannah had left the day before. But she did know that she felt very hungry. *I must have slept for several hours.* Light-headed, Denia took the pie pan containing a single slice of remaining pastry and put it in the oven to heat up. She then turned on the gas.

As was her morning custom Denia took the

handle of the coffee pot to move it to a burner. But as soon as she touched it the handle turned into a white snake and it began to coil up her forearm. The woman jerked her hand back. The snake rose in a mist and the apparition formed into the face of the shaman she had met by the wood. It said to her, "Nalusa Falaya!"

Denia was startled. She grabbed the pot of coffee once more and ran with it through the ell. As soon as she opened the screen door she tossed the pot over the railing of her back porch and into the grass.

The frightened woman stumbled back in and stood at the kitchen basin. She gazed out of the window staring at the dark silhouette of the Angel's Trumpets in full bloom. She thought of Moonshine and then she thought of the elixir. *Is it true? Have I made it too strong?*

Denia felt a presence behind her. She turned and instantly recognized the face. "You!" she cried, and a large shadowy hand grabbed her by the throat.

Denia scratched at the perpetrator's face. She struggled free and tried to exit around the table but fell. She struck the figure again with her fist but could not tell if she had missed or if it had grazed through him. This time a carving knife fell to the floor. She grabbed the dagger as the dark figure crouched over her. As the black mass tried to wrench her up by the arm she blindly swung wildly and yelled, "Sam! No!"

Denia released the grip on the blade. The man heaved her up and slammed the back of her head against the corner of the pie safe. There he let her body fall limp to the floor. Sam Hobbes slumped across from her—his blood dripped into a pool of spilled milk.

GHOSTS OF LEAF RIVER

"Those crows are going to be the death of Denia," Hannah said to her husband as she prepared to freshen up his cup of coffee.

"No thanks, dear—I've had enough," the man said refusing her offer. The man stepped away from the table, walked into the dining room, and peeked out of the window. "I thought you said she would probably drink herself to death," he called back to the kitchen.

"Well that too," Hannah said as she joined her voyeur husband.

A dim light shone in Denia's house. Hannah knew it was coming from the kitchen; the remainder of the house was still dark. Even the murder of crows gathering on her friend's lawn were in silhouette.

"I'll be off, Darlin'. I wanna get the crew

started early this morning." The man kissed his wife and squeezed her in a familiar way. She smiled back at him.

"OK. I'm going to get started on that persimmon butter with Denia before she gets so tipsy that we can't finish up again," Hannah added.

The two parted at the backdoor. As the man began walking to his truck he stopped, turned back to his wife, and said, "Looks like old Sam is early. I can see Oscar by his wagon out at Denia's. Hope you got some more of those lemon drops!" He smiled.

Hannah waved her husband on with a dishcloth in her hand. *At least Sam will be coming soon so I can pay him* she thought. The woman then returned to finish cleaning the breakfast dishes.

The sun rose as Hannah finished scrubbing the black iron skillets. She wiped down the stove and then sat down to finish off her cup of tea. As she sat there she thought to herself, *Sam sure is taking long over there. I really need to get going.*

After waiting a few more minutes Hannah decided that she would pay her debt at Denia's house. She wanted to get the day started and she *did not have time to wait on the store's hired help.* The restless young woman grabbed her sweater and marched out of the door.

Hannah made her way around to the front of her lawn. As she crossed the street toward her friend's home she could see Oscar still standing in front of his wagon patiently waiting for his master. Then she smelled something odd. It was if something was burning; and it came from the direction of Denia's house.

The woman suddenly became concerned and started to run. When she crossed the street at the edge of the front yard, the gathering of crows scattered into a black blur of swarming discontent. Their angry caws affirmed their disturbed feast.

Hannah raced up the back porch steps. She called *Denia? Denia!* before she flung open the screen door. Wisps of black smoke drifted in an already hazy kitchen.

"Denia!" Hannah screamed. She hopped over a box of scattered dry goods and a milk bottle that had been knocked sideways to reach her friend lying by the pie safe. She shook the woman on the floor but she did not respond. Hannah then turned to the stove. Smoke was puffing from the oven door. When Hannah opened it a bellow of char whisked out revealing an orange flicker from deep within. She slammed it shut and then turned the gas off with the oven's dial.

The frightened woman ran to the phone in the hallway. "Operator! Operator! Call Sheriff Henry."

Hannah looked back into the smoky kitchen. She could see Sam Hobbes lying across from her friend. "Tell him to get to Denia Andersen's house right away. I think that *nigrah* Sam Hobbes killed her. Hurry!"

After the instructions had been confirmed Hannah hung up the phone. She first opened all of the windows in the lower part of the house; then the kitchen ones. She was careful not to step on the scattered mess at her feet. When the smoke started to clear Hannah took a dish towel and grabbed the hot pie pan from the oven. She went outside to place the burnt slice of pecan pie on the back steps. That is when she noticed the coffee pot overturned in the grass.

It had taken the Sheriff the better part of an hour to get to Denia's home. On his way in from Collins, a deputy had stopped at the leading officer's home to tell him about the call. Sheriff Albert Henry and Doc Ellis had been in the pasture looking over a broken fence line between their two properties. A wanton bull had made little work of the barrier to exercise his desires over one of the physician's cows. It had taken time to collect the them.

When the two lawmen's cars skidded into Denia's pebble driveway, Hannah was sitting on the back porch—her eyes red. Doc Ellis had ridden in with the Sheriff; he hurried close in line behind the officers.

"What is it, Hannah?" Albert asked. "What's happened?"

"Denia's in there on the floor in the kitchen. And Sam Hobbes has a knife stuck in his side."

The three men rushed in to view the scene. It smelled of smoke and one corner of the room was in disarray. Sheriff Henry dashed to Denia's side first but the older doctor pushed him out of his way and began to examine her. The deputy inspected the delivery man as the sheriff stood back more concerned with the condition of the girl.

"She's had a bad rap to the back of her head. She's breathing; but looks like it's a concussion. I don't see anything else. We need to get her into bed and I can do a better examination of her. Let's put her on that couch first," the physician said. Albert Henry picked up the lifeless woman and moved her to the parlor.

While the Sheriff was tending to Denia the doctor examined the black man.

"Doesn't look like the knife went in too far. More like he has a busted eye; and they're wide open—all wild like. Broken nose too," the man assessed. "Not sure what this brown bubbly drool is. Kinda smells like…I don't know what. Tabacca? Liquor?"

After a few more moments of examining the unconscious man the doctor proclaimed, "Well, he'll live. Seems like he may have had a heart attack—but he's breathin'. And that knife wound isn't serious. I think he's just drunk."

Albert Henry was still by Denia's side when the medic came into the parlor. Doc Ellis noticed the red swell in the younger man's eyes. This time he gently urged the sheriff to the side.

After a thorough preliminary examination the physician said, "She has a few bruises but I think she's gonna be fine once she wakes up. We could take her to the hospital in Laurel but I think she might do better at home."

Hannah had come into the room to check on her friend moments earlier. "I can watch after her. I'll stay with her here."

"I can stay," Albert interjected. "I want

to be here when she wakes up."

Hannah and the doctor looked at each other. "That might be a couple days, Albert," the physician stated.

"That's OK," he replied. I wanna be here."

Hannah refrained from comment with her officious nature but instead said, "I'll help you. I'll make sure y'all have everything you need."

It was then agreed. Denia would remain in her home to recover and Sheriff Albert Henry would stay to watch over her. Hannah would tend to the house and the personal needs of her friend. And Sam Hobbes would go to jail in Collins to recover from his wounds. Doc Ellis saw no reason to take him to Charity Hospital in Laurel.

They moved Denia back upstairs into her bedroom. Hannah made a place for the Sheriff in an adjacent one across from hers. When they were assured of the ill woman's comfort, the two returned to the kitchen to clean up the mess.

"I don't understand this," Hannah started, "I know old Sam may have snuck a peek at us girls from time to time—they all do; but generally he was trustworthy. I never let him inside of my house with me. Denia did though."

"Well the way I see it ol' Sam Hobbes decided to have his way with her; she paid the price for it with a good rap on the head when she didn't oblige. Lucky enough he was drinkin' and she was able to put a knife in him. Maybe we *should* have a lynching in Cracker's Neck. Case is cut and dried," the sheriff said with disgust.

The two fumbled about collecting dish towels and a broom before deciding on how to start the clean up. Hannah knelt down by a spread of coffee grounds at the edge of the pie safe where Denia's feet had rested earlier. They were between the cabinet and a pool of pink stained milk.

"Looks like Denia was gonna make some of her award winning persimmon butter," the sheriff commented. She musta been ready to cut the persimmons with that knife she stuck that boy with. Lucky she had it close by."

"I reckon so," Hannah replied. But then she thought *why would Denia use a big ol' carving knife to cut up persimmons; a paring knife should have done the job.*

Hannah began to sweep up the grounds. They felt a bit oily and then her fingers began to tingle when she brushed them into the dustpan barehanded. She looked at the grit closely—it felt odd.

"I didn't know so much went into making this butter. Cinnamon, star anise, juniper berries, cloves…no wonder Denia wins every year with her jams," the sheriff said after reading the recipe for the spice sachet. He was holding a towel preparing to mop up the spilled milk and blood.

Hannah stood up with the dust pan. She glanced at the puddle of warm milk. A fly had already found the blood mix and was supping at the edge of the pool on the floor. There was a crushed green pod that reminded her of okra near it. The seeds were brown. A sticky boot print had tracked through the milk and deposited a few more seeds along the way.

"She has many secrets," Hannah said unwittingly.

The girl's fingers continued to itch. She considered where to dump the grounds as she glanced at the sachet on the butcher block table. And then she stopped.

What? she thought. "Albert. You said juniper berries?"

"Yep. That's what the recipe said," he responded while crouching down to clean the floor.

"Albert! Those aren't juniper berries!"

"Well that's what the recipe said," was his reply.

"No! On the table. These *are not* juniper berries," Hannah exclaimed. She looked into the dust pan and then to the crushed pod on the floor. "I think they're Angel's Trumpet seeds."

The sheriff stood up and looked at the open sachet on the table. He then looked at Hannah curiously and asked, "What is Denia doing cooking with that? It's poisonous."

"I don't know. But I don't think these are coffee grounds either!"

The sheriff looked into the pan. He pinched the pile then held it to his nose. "Doesn't smell like coffee."

"The pot! The coffee pot is outside in the grass," Hannah reported.

Sheriff Henry hurried outside to retrieve the tossed coffee vessel. He brought it back in and put it into the sink. By this time his fingers were starting to tingle.

"Hannah—get me a piece of newspaper."

The girl did as he was told. She also began to wipe her fingers onto a clean dish towel. Once Hannah had given the man the paper he knocked the grounds from the container and looked them over.

"I can't really tell but there are some

grounds that look a little darker and more irregular than the others," the sheriff said.

"These aren't coffee grounds. These are crushed up Angel's Trumpet seeds. Some of that stuff in the coffee pot looks like this in the dust pan. That's why my fingers itch. There's crushed up dried seeds in the coffee!" Hannah surmised.

"What the hell? Denia cooks with this stuff?" Albert questioned.

"*No*. I mean…I don't think so. I mean not with the seeds anyway," the girl defended.

"*Anyways?*" the sheriff inquired for clarification.

Hannah told the sheriff about Denia's elixir and the instruction she had received as a child from her mother. He was surprised to hear the tale. Albert Henry had no idea about this part of Denia's life. He had loved her since childhood and never had a clue about her obscure home life. He wondered what else he did not know about her.

Albert and Hannah talked long into the afternoon while cleaning the kitchen. They discussed their childhood together and reminisced about how long they had all known each other. Both agreed that the three of them had met early on in their elementary years at school.

Albert said he could not remember a time not knowing Denia. But Hannah recalled that their friend's family had moved to town in the middle of the first school year. Hannah and Denia had become best friends quickly. Albert confided that he had been in love with her from the beginning; but despite that and through all the years he was too shy to tell her. He never told his best friend Jonathon about it either, not even when they were to be married. The two also spoke of Adeline Skald.

"Addy Skrool? Yeah I remember her. She was as wild and mean as an old snake," the sheriff reminisced.

"She still is. Remember, she never came to school much? None of those Skalds did. Then she married her cousin. They all still live across the river up in Cracker's Neck. My daddy always told me they were carpetbaggers and trash. Even the Negroes and the Redbones wouldn't have anything to do with their kind. She hates Denia."

"Yeah, she mentioned that. But I can't figure out why," Albert said.

"Well. She blames Denia for stealing Jonathon away from her. I don't know how she figures that—Jonathon would never have had anything to do with her kind of mongrel breeding. She also told Denia once about how *sorry* she was that he had been killed in the accident. Denia thinks her husband Silas had something to do with it—Addy commented on how he *was* the only witness."

"I remember that day, Hannah. But nothing was ever questioned about it. I think it was just unfortunate that the chains broke loose. At the rate they cut trees around here logging accidents happen all the time."

"Well, I don't know. But I sure think she hates Denia enough to try and kill her. I'm not sure that old Sam did try to hurt her. Just doesn't make sense—that drunk that early in the morning and all? He might have been poisoned; and what about that coffee pot and the grounds on the floor? Doesn't make sense. Did you know she soaks her grounds overnight?" Hannah further detailed.

Sheriff Albert Henry listened to the woman's new conspiracy theories but he had already made his mind up. *Sam Hobbes had attacked his long beloved and that was that.* Any other pertinent information would have to come from the witness; and she was still sleeping.

The first night the sheriff had stayed with Denia was mostly uneventful. She mumbled a few times about shadow people and spoke in a way that Albert thought she may have been speaking in tongues. But throughout the early morning hours he sat in a chair by her side. He never left her and he never slept in the bed that Hannah had prepared for him in the other room.

The following morning Hannah came by to prepare breakfast for the sentry and also to care for her invalid friend. She brought a pot of fresh hot coffee over after her husband left for work. Hannah knew the sheriff drank several cups a day and that he had not had any in the past few hours. The cunning girl was also keen not to have made it with any of Denia's beans.

"Thank you for the coffee, Hannah," the sheriff said while pouring himself a cup of the black elixir.

"You're welcome, Albert. I hope it's as good as Denia's," she said with a sly smile.

Albert Henry looked up from the table at Hannah as she placed a plate of country scrambled eggs, fried jowl bacon, and some left over biscuits in front of him—all cooked at her house. When his lips touched the rim of the coffee cup he thought, *and how well do I know this smiling face?*

"Hannah. I thought a little about what you said last night. Is there anything else you can remember about yesterday? Something you haven't told me?" the lawman inquired.

He had not meant to sound interrogating but Hannah replied, "As in you think I may have had something to do with my friend's demise?"

The man stopped chewing. It interrupted his more pressing thought of how good the fresh eggs tasted having been cooked in the bacon grease.

She noticed his surprise. "That's alright, Sheriff. I'd be offended if you didn't inquire about all the possibilities."

"Hannah—I didn't mean..."

"It's OK," she reassured.

"Last night Denia mumbled something about shadow men. And she called out for Jonathon and also for you. I think she was speaking in tongues as well. I really couldn't understand, but one thing I did hear was something like *nasue-fasue, nal-ya faya*...or something like that. I don't know but it sounded familiar in some way or something.

"Nalusa Falaya, I think. It's the Choctaw name for some kind of a ghost or dark

shadowy like man she told me about," Hannah said.

"What ghost?" the man further inquired.

"Oh I don't know. Denia drinks that tonic I told you about. I think it makes her drunk. She said sometimes she sees shadow people at night. I think it's that Redbone, Choctaw Indian that she gets it from," she said in a glib way.

Hannah had amused herself in a facetious way. Then she became serious.
"The rider. I saw a *rider* yesterday morning when I ran up to the house."

"Who was it?" the sheriff asked.

"Well, I don't know. But he was on a horse galloping into the woods out by where Denia picks her persimmons. He was heading toward the swamp. I just thought it was a hunter."

"You didn't see who it was?"

"No. But it could have been that Addy Skrool!" Hannah exclaimed.

"Why would it be her? They live up in Cracker's Neck—Jones County across the river a-ways," the sheriff stated.

"Hey, y'all," a voice called from behind them.

"Hey Doc," the sheriff answered back while turning around in his chair.

"I thought I'd get started early and check on my patient," the doctor announced. "Any changes?"

The doctor and the lawman briefly chatted while Hannah went upstairs to prepare Denia for another exam. When she had finished the three caretakers proceeded with the task at hand and developed an immediate care plan. They told the medical examiner about the Angel's Trumpet elixir and the coffee.

When he had finished the observation, Doc Ellis pronounced that Denia was *faring well* and that the two sitters should continue on as needed. Should anything change they were to call the physician immediately. The doctor attributed Denia's unconscious verbalization as the affects of poisoning. He said they should wear off in time. He also said she most likely had been hallucinating from the scopolamine contained in the plant.

As the day wore on Albert Henry stayed with Denia. Hannah twice more brought food for the loyal man. He would not leave the house and mostly sat by her side reading whatever was available. That night he again fell asleep in the chair next to her.

Denia's dreams were fitful. She dreamt of two girls in the woods; they appeared lost. A

small man the size of a child found them and
led them to a cave with three old men sat
around a fire. One man offered the girls a knife.
One offered them a bound bundle of poisonous
leaves. Yet another offered the girls a basket of
healing herbs. One of the girls grabbed the
knife and ran away. The other girl chose the
basket of herbs and stayed with the faceless
men. Their long white hair never revealed their
bowed brows.

In her dreams she also saw dogs lying
dead on the forest floor. It was if she were
looking through a child's eyes. Shadows moved
about the woods. Lights floated over the river;
and *fish-people* beckoned her to come closer to
the water's edge. In the distance she saw what
appeared to be a beaver dam. And she also saw
a headless man on the banks of the river fishing
with a spear.

Before the dawn broke Denia woke from
her fitful sleep. "*Bohpoli!*" she screamed into
the night.

Albert Henry tumbled out of his chair
and onto the floor with a crash. His heart beat
as if it were to fly off like a scared crow. He
was not sure but he thought he may have wet
himself; a now empty water glass rolled behind
him.

"Denia? Denia, it's Albert," he addressed as he regained his composure.

The girl's eyes were wild and wide in the waning moonlight. The sight of him gave her a fright though arguably not as much as she had him. But the jarring moment helped to jolt her from the waking haze of sleep.

"Albert? Albert! What are you doing here?"

The sheriff turned on the bedside lamp and assured her of his intentions. He briefly explained to her what had occurred in past days. When she was satisfied with his explanation Denia was grateful for his company. She also became engaged with his compassionate touch. It was a feeling she had not felt physically or emotionally in a long time. It comforted her. He said he would not soon leave her side.

Albert helped as she drank from the replenished water glass. She needed to hydrate and willingly accepted. The two chatted of things past and present until a soft morning light filled the room.

"Albert. There are things you must know. Things about Addy Skald." Denia then told the sheriff what she had seen in her dream prophecy and elaborated on her nemesis' cruelty.

The man listened to her story. But he dismissed much of it as the affects from the poison. He was not sure how much credibility she had insinuating that Addy Skald was a *demon* that was trying to kill her. Besides, he didn't much believe in the old Indian tales and superstitions that he had heard over the years— and Sam Hobbes was still his prime suspect in attacking her.

"Sam Hobbes saved my life! I'm telling you that Silas Skald came out of the shadows and grabbed me in the kitchen. I scratched at his face and when he bent down to grab me again, a knife must have gotten knocked out of his coat and I grabbed it."

Denia started to cry. "But when he jerked me up and I swung the blade—old Sam was behind him trying to get that trash off of me. That's all I remember."

Albert Henry could not deny that the facts reported by the victim were a possibility. Even though some of Denia's story sounded more like a tall tale from an intoxicated woman, the physical evidence was credible as presented. He started to reconstruct the scene in his head. And Hannah's theory of Addy poisoning Denia made more sense. *But were she and Silas the mysterious shadow people? Maybe its time to visit Addy Skald* he thought.

Sheriff Henry waited for Hannah and Doc Ellis to arrive. Both were elated to see the patient awake and doing well. After the doctor had given Denia a good report on her condition Albert asked Hannah if she wouldn't mind staying with her for the day. She joyfully agreed and the sheriff made plans from Denia's home for the trip to Addy's abode in Cracker's Neck.

The lawman prepared for the worst. He called for two of his deputies to meet him at the crime scene, and also arranged for his farm hand to bring horses, hounds, and supplies to the livery at Herbert's Store. The sheriff then called ahead to have his friend and Jones County Sheriff meet them at Reddoch's Ferry. He would have two men as well.

That should be enough lawmen if there's any trouble with the Skald clan Albert thought. They didn't have a warrant, but knowing the Skalds they wouldn't need one if their guilty ways prompted them to fighting. The plan was to question Adeline Skald. It was not to arrest her for anything—not yet.

The posse arrived near the Skald place just before noon. The men were greeted by lines of large leathery skulls, in various degrees of decay, belonging to catfish and sturgeon that were impaled upon sun-baked fence posts. The main house was a rough-hewn cabin; several out buildings sprawled around it. Chord woven fishing nets and a rotten dugout pirogue littered the dusty space. An overgrown empty corral with a propped up broken gate gave the only open reception to the deserted yard as they slowly drove in.

Sheriff Henry was the first to honk his car horn. Signaling the arrival of company in the country was not only a sign of respect, it also kept one from being shot as a trespasser. But when he opened his door to exit the vehicle a barrage of bullets greeted the officers.

It was a typical Skald welcoming. That is why the lawmen always entered in a staggered formation with engines pointing forward. They immediately backed up. Bullets flew into the Covington County Sheriff's engine and shot out the radiator. Despite it all, Albert Henry was able to maneuver his car into a defensive sideways position to give cover for the rest of the men. He then jumped out with revolver in hand.

The lawman fired back. The shots seemed to have been fired from the cover of tall thin pines near the corral. Then the cabin door burst open and a woman with a shotgun fired at the lone sheriff. It did not take long before Henry's friend and the other deputies eased up next to him and returned fire into house and the woods.

Trees splintered in all forward directions. After a moment the shooting stopped but the cabin door remained cracked open. Horse's hooves could be heard galloping toward the river behind the house. All became eerily quiet. Only the chilly breeze in the tops of the trees could be heard from above. The blue azure sky was clear without a single cloud.

"What cha' thinkin', Albert?" his friend asked. "Gonna give it a go and see what's left inside."

"Reckon we better. Ain't gonna get any better a welcome than that," Sheriff Henry chuckled. "I'll take my boys up front and you go around with yours to the back. Y'all have more cover that way."

Sheriff Henry and his men charged in turn to the front of the cabin. When they had all reached the door the sheriff kicked it open the remainder of the way. The interior was smoky and stunk like burnt dried leaves and river water. It was not a tidy place. Wood chips were littered in front of the hearth. A hatchet lay on the floor.

The other lawmen came in through the back. They reported that the Skalds had most likely made a run to the river behind them.

"Well, they can't go through the quarters. Those Negroes and Redbones don't want them up there. I suspect they're headin' for the swamp back north of Hot Coffee," Sheriff Henry stated.

One of the Jones County deputies said, "Hey Sheriff—look at here." He was in the kitchen.

Both of the senior lawmen left the living area to have a look. The kitchen was as cluttered as the front of the house. Dirty wet overalls were draped over a chair. Freshly cut fish carcasses lay in the sink. A black iron skillet full of dirty cooking oil rested on the wood stove.

Sheriff Henry noticed an open cupboard with a sack of spilled cornmeal. A large brown palmetto bug raced for cover. "Guess we interrupted their dinner," he said.

"Yes, sir. But what's this you think?" the deputy questioned peeking into a small, dark, pantry-like space on the other side of the kitchen wall. There was an amber glow coming from the narrow covey.

"Have a look, Albert," the man's friend said.

Sheriff Henry peeked inside. "Good Lord. That's Jonathan Andersen."

As the lawman assessed what he was looking at he was able to identify a picture of Denia's husband. It was illuminated by a crude, pine-pitch candle. There was also a mirror, a hairbrush, a bundle of leaves, some seed pods and something reflecting with a gold tint and red sparkle.

The man reached inside and pulled out a ring. He recognized it immediately. There was no other like it in the county. It was gold with interlocking circles and two small, ruby red stones. It was Denia's wedding ring.

Albert took the remaining personal items from the pigeonhole. He thought again about what Denia and Hannah had said about Addy. *Maybe they were right about her* he thought.

"We gotta get back across the river. Can you and your boys stay on this side and hold them off if they try to cross again?"

"Sure Albert. I'll see if I can't get a few more men over here," the Jones County Sheriff promised. "You gonna be OK over there?"

"Yeah. I got my tracker and some horses

ready on the other side. I'm just gonna grab the shotgun out my car and I'll ride back with my boys. We outta be able ta' get 'em before the swamp gets too dark."

"Well take care, Albert. We'll handle this side. I'll send word up to the quarters that the Skalds are on the run—if they don't already know. No love lost there; they won't be passin' that way. You take the swamp and we'll cover the river downstream. Good luck."

With that the men parted. Sheriff Henry and his team crossed back over Reddoch's Ferry and reorganized at Herbert's livery. By the time they left for the swamp they estimated they still had at least four hours of good light left. It was a concern but with the dogs they thought they could at least get them cornered; after all, *there was only so far that the Skalds could travel into the depths of the swamp* the men thought.

It wasn't but a couple of miles in that the forest turned into swamp. The logging roads ended and the brush became thick with bear grass and briar. Deer trails in the soggy ground soon became the preferred method of passage as they traveled farther in. The horses eventually had to navigate farther from the path into the slew. The trees thickened and the canopy allowed less light in.

The men began to hear the dogs howl more excitedly after the third hour in. Nearby the caw of a crow warned others to beware. Along the way they had seen deer, turkey, and hogs scatter around them. But the only thing that might distract the hounds was a bear or a panther. The men, however, were alert to the game animals that they had to pass by— opportunities lost on this expedition.

In the dimness the men now became more aware of the fading light. They thought tricks were being played on their eyes when flickers like lightning bugs had appeared from time to time before their path. It was curious. It was too cold and too late in the season for the insects to be fluttering about. They trudged on in the wet, sucking marsh.

"Sheriff. Is that cypress stump one we've seen before?" a deputy asked.

Albert looked where the man had pointed. "I don't think so. Whada' ya think Hank? Are we goin' in circles?" he asked the tracker.

"No. Stuff just looks like the same from

time to time. But the dogs have quieted down. And that concerns me more."

The Sheriff realized that it had been ten minutes or so since they had heard the steady howl of the beasts. Now it seemed as if only one distinct bark of the three dogs could be located. His was a slightly higher pitch than that of the two blood hounds. Only the Black and Tan bear hound named Murphy seemed audible—and he seemed to be staying in one spot. The men made way to his call.

"Damn it!" Hank shouted ahead of them. "It's Lulu. She's dead."

When the rest of the party reached the man they saw that the dog had a dark froth coming from her muzzle. Her eyes were wide open. It reminded Sheriff Henry of how Sam Hobbes had been found.

"They poisoned her; bastards *poisoned* my old girl," he repeated.

The men hurried in the direction of Murphy's last bray. But not more than twenty yards from Lulu's body was also her sister Betty. The dog had succumbed to the same fate. Hank was enraged and he cursed the Skalds on their mother's grave.

The light was now fading fast. Shadows seemed to appear and disappear behind distant trees. It worried Albert about *just how many Skalds were out there.* At last count he knew that there were at least five including Addy. But he doubted that she was with them in the swamp. *It was no place for a woman.*

The woods grew even quieter. Lights danced in the distance and the men thought that the flickers may have been lanterns or flashlights. But when they came upon the body of *ol' Murphy-dog* they were sure that the *flickers* had been closer.

The swamp was dark now and the sun had dipped well beneath the canopy of trees. Only a slither of red from the obstructed western sky caught the fading sunset in a single thin cloud above them.

"Damn its dark, Sheriff. We're gonna have to break out these flashlights," one of the deputies stated.

"Yeah I know," the senior lawman said. "Just use the red lens on them right now. We'll hit 'em with the spot beams if we see 'em. Don't we have two of those?"

"I got one with me," Hank said, his breath misting in the cool air.

"I've got the other," the deputy in the rear stated.

"Well, let's go. Move on up there toward

those lightning bugs or will-o-wisps or whatever they are," the Sheriff directed. They can't get much farther into the swamp. It's just too thick."

The men moved several more yards following what they thought were man-made lights. To their surprise the swamp began to widen and the trees were less numerous as if they had been logged out or at least thinned. And then they saw it. A twiggy mass in the dark nestled up against a pile of debris.

An amber glow gently reflected in a pool of liquid in front of the hut. The air smelled like the inside of the Skalds cabin—acrid and smoky. Hank and the men knew exactly what it was. But no beaver would start a fire inside his own home. They had tracked the clan to their final destination. And if they resisted arrest the swamp would be their grave.

"Let's get around the back of 'em boys," the sheriff whispered. "Then we'll fire a couple shots in if they don't wanna come out. Tie your horses up here."

The posse did as instructed and left the four horses secured in a considered amount of yards from the beaver's lodge. As they neared the den the men could see where the Skalds had dug out an opening on one side for an egress.

The light from the fire inside reflected onto the wet mud before it.

Suddenly shots rang out. The lawmen took cover behind stumps. The only indication of where the bullets had been fired from was the muzzle flash. But the direction was not even close to the hut's location. Splashing water in the dark gave an indication to where the fugitives had fled to—and it was behind the men.

"Get the horses, Hank!" the sheriff shouted. "You boys check out the hut and make sure nobody else is in there!"

Each man did as ordered. Albert saw a shadow race by him but there seemed to be no sound. He told himself that it was the adrenaline pumping through his body that silenced his hearing. He took chase regardless splashing behind in the chilly water.

Albert became concerned when the water began to get deeper and deeper. When it got up his knees he turned back with gun in hand. After a few dozen yards Albert recognized Hank holding the horses not far from him in the other direction. The red lens on his flashlight was shining toward hooves on the ground.

"Hank! Hank!" the sheriff shouted. "The swamp widens over here. I think we're not too far from the river. Gimme my horse—and my shotgun," the lawman demanded as he approached the man.

The tracker left the three other horses secured to the tree limbs and met the sheriff halfway with his animal. Albert took the reigns, jumped on and said, "Get those boys mounted and let's go after 'em. The Skalds are on foot. We gotta get to 'em before they get to the boats!"

Hank trudged back and Albert took off into the watery brush. But as soon as the tracker got to the horses a small, dark, child-like figure made one of them rear up. It knocked the man down. The spooked horse took off into the direction of the swamp's thicket. The two remaining deputies got there in time to calm down the remaining two mares.

Sheriff Henry splashed through the muck in pursuit of the fugitives. The ground began to turn less watery and drier than before until a defined bank emerged. It was then that shots rang out once more. Albert jumped from his horse and ran to the cover of the outlying pines. He could see four shapes of men running down a slither of land by a wide spot in the river.

Damn—we were right across from Cracker's Neck Albert thought. The sheriff fired several shots from his revolver in the direction of the Skalds. In a few moments the rest of his men arrived by his side.

"I think we got 'em pinned down. I don't see the boats, but I don't wanna stick my head up and get it shot off either," the sheriff said excitedly. "Hank, you come with me and you boys go up the bank a bit and see if you can get a better angle on 'em. We'll try to get them to run down a bit away from their boats in case they have any over here."

The men split up. Albert and Hank noticed the lightning bugs fluttering over the water again. That's when the four Skalds made a run for it and scurried down the slither of beach along cover of the high bank. Sheriff Henry could see the tops of their heads. But he also saw black figures standing on the other side of the river's bank. He inferred that the lights reflecting on the river's surface where the flashlights from the Jones County Sheriff lawmen in the distance.

"Let's get 'em, Hank!"

The men had not stood and taken more than three steps when Albert saw a muzzle flash from the beach. He did not hear it but felt a whiz rush past his ear. The sheriff did, however, hear Hank cry out in a mournful chirp as the bullet caught him in the neck and knocked him to the ground. Albert dropped down again. A barrage of rifle fire ensued from the upper river bank where the deputies had taken position. Albert grabbed the shotgun next to Hank. Then splashes were heard in the water.

"Let 'em go boys! Sheriff's gonna get 'em on the other side. Rivers too wide for 'em ta' get out quick," Albert hollered. "I got 'em on this side. Come back down this way!"

Sheriff Henry stood up with the shotgun and ran along the river bank. Water sloshed in his boots; his feet were numb. He was watching the figures in the river when something hard and swift swiped his foot out from under him. He fell over the man-high bank and face forward onto the beach landing on top of his gun. When he rolled over a man stabbed him in the left shoulder with a cypress fishing spear. He knew the man's face even in the dark.

Silas Skald pulled the wooden spear out of Albert's shoulder. The sheriff kicked the man's feet out from under him. Albert curled up and reached blindly for his gun. Silas regained his composure onto his knees in the sand and grasped the spear with both hands. As the outlaw began his thrust at Albert's chest, the sheriff slung his shotgun at Addy's husband's throat and pulled both triggers. The double barrel blast blew Silas Skald's head clean off his neck and into the river.

Sheriff Henry was not sure if what he saw next over that river was the flash in his eyes from the blast or lightning bugs, but he did hear the screams. The men who had tried to cross the river were now swimming and splashing back toward him. Not a one made it.

Albert and his men witnessed something odd. It appeared that the swimmers had spooked a giant sturgeon or catfish in the river. One by one they were pulled down to their death. Only the reflection of a leathery pale skin and huge flailing splashes gave clues that it could not have been anything else. After all, proof of one of these 200 pound beasts had been caught, stuffed, and was currently displayed in Herbert's Store.

The sheriff got up from his ordeal. Although the puncture wound was deep, the cold helped to anesthetize it. He climbed up the river bank and checked on his men. When he looked back, the dark figures across the river started to quietly disperse.

"How's Hank? How bad is it?"

"He's alive. But he's bleeding. I think the bullet went clean through his neck. But he's sittin' up holdin' a rag around it," a deputy said.

"We found the boats too," the other reported.

"Hey there, Albert! How y'all doing? We heard the shootin'. Y'all get them boys?" the Jones County lawman shouted from across the way. Their spot flashlights lit up the river water and its banks.

"What'er you talkin' about? Silas is dead. Didn't y'all see those three other boys drown in the river?" Albert shouted back.

"We just got here. Heard the gunfire from the cabin. It's only a hundred yards or so from here."

Albert Henry and his men looked at each other confused.

"Well, I got a man down. Can ya' take him to Laurel?"

"Yeah! You got a boat over there?" they cried back.

"Yeah! We'll send him over," Albert confirmed.

The second deputy ran off to fetch the fugitive's skiff. Albert sat and rested with the remaining officer and Hank.

"Where's the fourth horse?" Albert inquired.

"It spooked and ran off into the woods,"

the man replied.

Sheriff Henry rested in thought for a moment. He recalled the dead dogs; he remembered the bundle of leaves in the cabin. Men had drowned in the river in a most peculiar way, and—*a headless man on the banks of the river fishing with a spear.*

"Denia!" the sheriff shouted. And he jumped up. "I gotta get to the house."

Sheriff Henry took one of the horses and dry bullets for his revolver. He gave instruction for the deputies to get Hank across the river and then bring the horses back to Denia's as soon as they could; but to *ride together.*

It did not take Albert long to find the logging road. Once he made it to Herbert's Store he cut across to Denia's.

When he reached her house it was dark with the exception of the kitchen light. As he dismounted Albert heard a horse whinny near the collard patch. The horse walked into the light shining from the ell's window when he called to it. It was the one that had run through the swamp. The animal was muddy, sweaty, and looked like it had been ridden hard through briar and thicket. Albert rushed up the back steps with his hand on his pistol.

"Hannah! Hannah!" he cried. There was

no answer.

A teapot sat on the block table in the kitchen. It had hot water steaming from it and a tea tin was nearby. An empty porcelain cup rested on the counter and he noticed that another was shattered into pieces on the floor.

Albert bolted toward the staircase in the dark. The waxing gibbous moonlight in the clear sky had started to give some illumination in the night through the tree tops. The bluish haze crept in by window and onto the stairs as the sheriff made his way to Denia's bedroom.

When he flung the door open he could see Denia sitting on the edge of the bed. A trickle of black blood ran down the side of her neck. Her pale, reflecting, white skin showed it all. Addy was holding the blade tight against her throat.

"I will have my revenge! I see how you feel for her. She stole my Jonathon and neither he nor you will ever have her now. I will kill her just like I did our parents! And the others! My sister will pay for what she's done to me!" she screamed in a rant.

The sheriff was confused. "*Sister*? What are you *talking* about, Addy? Put that knife down!" Albert demanded as he pointed his revolver at her.

"Tell him sister. Tell him our secrets!" Addy hissed as she hid behind Denia. There was no way Albert could get a good shot off— *yet*. The wild eyed woman may have seemed mad but she still had some sense of strategy.

"She says she's my twin sister Daniyah. We were lost in the woods when we were young. Our parents moved us here from Louisiana. We had family that lived in the quarters above Cracker's Neck. So we moved there with the Melungeon families. Some call them Redbones. But I am neither. My parents are Isleño and Slav—outcasts all the same. Isn't that enough, Addy?"

"Our parents you mean! Tell them why they left me with the Skalds!"

"*Our parents*!" Denia cried as the knife bore into her skin. Albert tried to position himself but Addy pulled the knife tighter.

"Drop that gun or I'll cut her throat!"

"Not until you put that knife down, Addy," the sheriff demanded.

"Ah, yes. The knife. Tell him that part sister."

"When we were in the woods," Denia started with a gulp, "we were playing and catching lightning bugs as our parents picked Mayhaw berries near the swamp. We were

about five years old. But they were not
lightning bugs at all. The Choctaw call them
Hashok Okwa Huiga—grass water drop. Some
call them will-o'-wisps. And they lead those
who enter into the swamp in circles to be lost.
They also lure boys to *Bohpoli* who help train
them as medicine men."

"*Bohpoli?* I've heard you say that before
in your dreams," Albert said.

"Yes," Denia continued. "They are small
forest dwellers. They steal children and lead
them to the three old shaman who offer a knife,
poisonous leaves, or healing herbs to the child."
Denia's voice crackled.

"Tell him!" Addy squealed as she pulled
the captive's hair backward. Denia's neck
began to smear red.

"If he takes the poison he will never be
able to make good medicine. If he takes the
herbs he will be a healer and able to help his
clan. If he takes the knife—"

"Yes! If he takes the knife he will be an
abomination like *me*, Sister! But I took the
knife because I was afraid. And I ran into the
wood without you. And the water drops led me
to the Skalds and they keep me prisoner there!
And mother and father never looked for me! So
I poisoned Mother's coffee by night and killed

Father in the woods just like I had Silas kill
Jonathon!"

"That's not true! They did look for you.
For months! When the Bohpoli sent me back,
they searched the woods but they never could
find you. We moved to town when Father got
promoted with the logging company. We never
stopped looking for you. Then I started school.
I never knew you were my sister until now—
you never told me! You hardly ever came! You
were always so mean to me and the other kids,"
Denia sobbed.

"Because I hate you! And I'm going to
kill you!" the deranged woman screamed.

"Jonathon!" Denia cried out in vain as
she closed her eyes.

But before another word was uttered a
tall figure from the corner shadows of the unlit
room swept behind Addy and grabbed her by
the chin. The hand of the dark form snapped her
head back with such an impact that there was a
resounding *POP!* Her arm shot forward as the
knife darted from her lifeless fingers and across
the room.

The commanding force of the black
figure continued in its backward motion.
Addy's body was lifted up by her dislodged
neck and thrown crashing through the bedroom

window. Glass and splinters of wooden window frame exploded with such violence that all of the shattered debris exited outside.

Sheriff Henry was stunned by the spectacle in front of him. The sparse moonlight in the dark room gave no clue as to who the man was as the shadowy apparition lurched past the lawman. He felt only as if a strong wind had passed straight through him.

Albert looked behind him as to capture the beings exit. Then he ran to the broken window. Addy Skrool had fallen on top of Denia's Angel's Trumpets—crushing them. Her head was ajar from her shoulders in a most grotesque way. Although her body was facing downward her head was cocked backward—her once vibrant green eyes now clouding grey.

Denia ran to Albert at the window. They hugged each other tight before the two gazed back out at the scene below on the lawn. A man was standing over Addy's body; a small dark figure hid behind a pecan tree in the shadows. When the taller figure looked up, Denia instantly recognized his long braids with bangs cropped above his eyebrows. He then turned and disappeared as if into a mist; but the night was clear.

"Thank you, Bohpoli," Denia said.

Albert looked back at her—into her eyes with yearning curiosity.

"Denia. Denia?" a weak voice said.

The two turned and looked to the doorway of the bedroom.

"Hannah!" the sheriff cried. "Did you see who ran down the stairs?"

"*I* came up the stairs. Someone knocked me out in the kitchen and I woke up in the parlor."

"No! Who ran down the stairs just now?" Albert demanded as he rushed toward her.

"No one. Just me," she said again.

"Hannah. Come sit down over here," Denia urged.

Albert took the girl by the arm and ushered her next to her friend on the bed.

"Oh, Denia. I'm so sorry. I didn't mean to—I mean I don't know what's happening here!" Sheriff Henry declared.

"I'm fine now that y'all are here," she replied squeezing Hannah's hand.

Then she pulled Albert down to sit on the bed next to her. She wrapped her arms around him.

"I'm not gonna let you go again so easily," Albert assured.

"I should hope not," Denia replied.

EPILOGUE

Sheriff Albert Henry had questions about what he and his men had seen and heard that night. But the sheriff fancied himself as being a fact and evidence based man. He came to terms that everything he had wondered about could be explained.

The "will-o'-wisps" were lightning bugs and reflections off of the water. The shadows in the woods were the Skalds eluding them behind trees. The gathered group of shadows on the river banks that he saw before his Sheriff friend arrived were Sam Hobbes' people and accompanying Redbones. They drove the men back into the water where they drowned from cold water cramps.

The mysterious shadowy rescuer in

Denia's room was her Choctaw friend. He threw Addy out of the window before bolting past him and Hannah while the two were still in shock. That *was a fact* because he had even seen the man standing over her dead body when they looked out of the window.

Concerning the "lost" twin sister story, the poison was still affecting Denia's mind. It made her hallucinate—just as Doc Ellis had said. And Addy Skald was just a crazy woman. Denia agreed to never speak of it again; Albert knew *it was best* for her.

Sam Hobbes *did* save Denia from Silas Skald—and for that he was released immediately the following day. Moonshine had been killed by a passing wagon, and the only other murders in Hot Coffee were solved by Addy Skald's own admission.

Anything else, Sheriff Albert Henry surmised, *was just plain old Indian folklore*— no matter what his newly betrothed may have said. And he didn't believe another word otherwise. However, a few months later, folks did say they saw a headless ghost fishing on the Leaf River. *But that is another story.*

The Spacek and Toussaint Mysteries

The Spacek and Toussaint Mysteries are a historical fiction novel series involving two journalists who investigate urban legends. Along the way they find more than they had expected including their own unknown pasts.

Onionhead is the first novel in the series—it should be in print by early 2017. It's major setting is a 1970's south Louisiana north of New Orleans around Lake Pontchartrain. The story of the Creoles, Choctaws, and an unsolved grisly murder from the 1920's are detailed around the mossy bayous and cemeteries of the region. A local legendary figure haunts the pages of this mystery and it is rumored that he still roams to this day—in real life! Is he immortal or just an urban legend?

The second novel in the series is *The Ghosts of Leaf River*. It should be available by the end of 2017. This story continues the adventures of Anthony Spacek and Amélie Toussaint which will lead them into another mystery in south Mississippi based on the more mature characters from the prequel novelette *Murder in Hot Coffee*; the Free State of Jones (a historical secession of neither Union nor Confederacy during the Civil War) and an enigmatic American opera singer of color who often performs in France will also make appearances.

ABOUT THE AUTHOR

Author KT Ashely is an American writer from the South whose genres include Historical, Realistic, and Mystery Fiction. He is a native of Louisiana but now lives in southern Mississippi. The author also lived for several years in northern New England after serving in the U.S. Naval Nuclear Submarine Force during the Cold War. Much of his writing is influenced by historical events from contemporary to ancient. The human condition and it's affects on society are often the theme. Plot lines involving prejudices, indifference, wealth disparities, and military service are common.

New short stories by the author are regularly posted on www.authorktashely.com for your free, reading enjoyment.